First published in 2015
by Jessica Kingsley Publishers
73 Collier Street
London N1 9BE, UK
and
400 Market Street, Suite 400
Philadelphia, PA 19106, USA

www.jkp.com

Library of Congress Cataloging in Publication Data
A CIP catalog record for this book is available from the Library of Congress

British Library Cataloguing in Publication Data
A CIP catalogue record for this book is available from the British Library

ISBN 978 1 84905 655 7
eISBN 978 1 78450 151 8

Printed and bound in Canada

The Princess and the FOG

A Story for Children with Depression

Written and illustrated by Lloyd Jones

With a contribution
by Melinda Edwards MBE and Dr Linda Bayliss

Jessica Kingsley *Publishers*
London and Philadelphia

Lloyd Jones is a silly man with a silly beard who lives in the south of England with his fiancée Hannah, to whom this book is dedicated. He has learned to live with his fog rather than suffer from it. More of his work can be seen at www.lloydjonesillustration.com.

Once upon a time,
there was a Princess.

She loved to read.

She loved to play outside
with her friends.

She loved school.

She loved to ride her horses.

She loved her loyal subjects.

She loved her mum and dad
(the King and Queen).

She was loved by all in turn, for she was smart, beautiful, brave, honest and kind.

She had everything a little girl could ever want, and she was happy.

That is, until the fog came.

It happened slowly.

So slowly that nobody really
noticed, at first.

One by one, the strange, dark clouds came to the Princess, following her and gradually gathering around her head.

As time went on, it got worse and worse.

The clouds kept gathering and growing.

Eventually her whole head was surrounded by a deep,
dark fog that she could hardly see out of any more.

But still nobody noticed.

She started to feel completely
alone, even when she wasn't.

The fog made the Princess feel slow, sad and tired.

She had trouble concentrating on or doing
even the simplest of things.

Suddenly everything seemed really difficult.

All the things she used to love to do, she suddenly didn't feel like doing any more.

So she just stopped doing them.

Finally, the King and Queen began to see the fog.
They wanted to help the princess,
but didn't know how.

They tried to get rid of the fog,
but it wouldn't go away.

The King and Queen just wanted the Princess to be happy, but nothing could stop her from feeling sad.

They didn't know what to do,
but they kept trying.

One day, a friend from school came to the castle to ask the Princess if she wanted to go out and play.

But the Princess didn't feel like playing.

She didn't feel like doing anything.

The next day, her friend came to the castle again
to ask the Princess if she wanted to read comics together.

But the Princess didn't feel like reading comics.

She didn't feel like doing anything.

The day after that, her friend came back again
to ask the Princess if she wanted
to watch some TV together.

But the Princess didn't feel like watching TV.

So her friend asked the
Princess if she wanted to talk.

At first, the Princess wasn't sure. She found it difficult
and didn't know what to say. But, little by little,
she began to talk. The Princess found that the more
she talked about the fog, the better she felt.

So they talked and talked and talked.
They talked all night, but she still had more to say.

She talked to her
other friends

and she talked
to her parents.

She talked to
her teacher

and anyone else
who would listen.

Some just listened, but some had similar things to say.
Some of them even had ideas of ways they could help.

Her teacher told her to go and see the
Adventurers, who took her exploring
in the fresh air and sunshine.

They also helped her set daily challenges for herself.

Completing a challenge every day helped her to feel healthier and happier.

The King and Queen took her
to see the castle Druid. They talked
about the fog, and he brewed up
some potions for her to try.

Her friends told her about the 1000-Year-Old Wise Woman, who told her that fog like this had been seen in the Kingdom before.

It often followed people who felt sad
or lonely, or had been treated badly.

But sometimes it came for no obvious reason at all.

It isn't easy to make the fog go away, but it helps to talk
about it and do the things that make you feel happy.

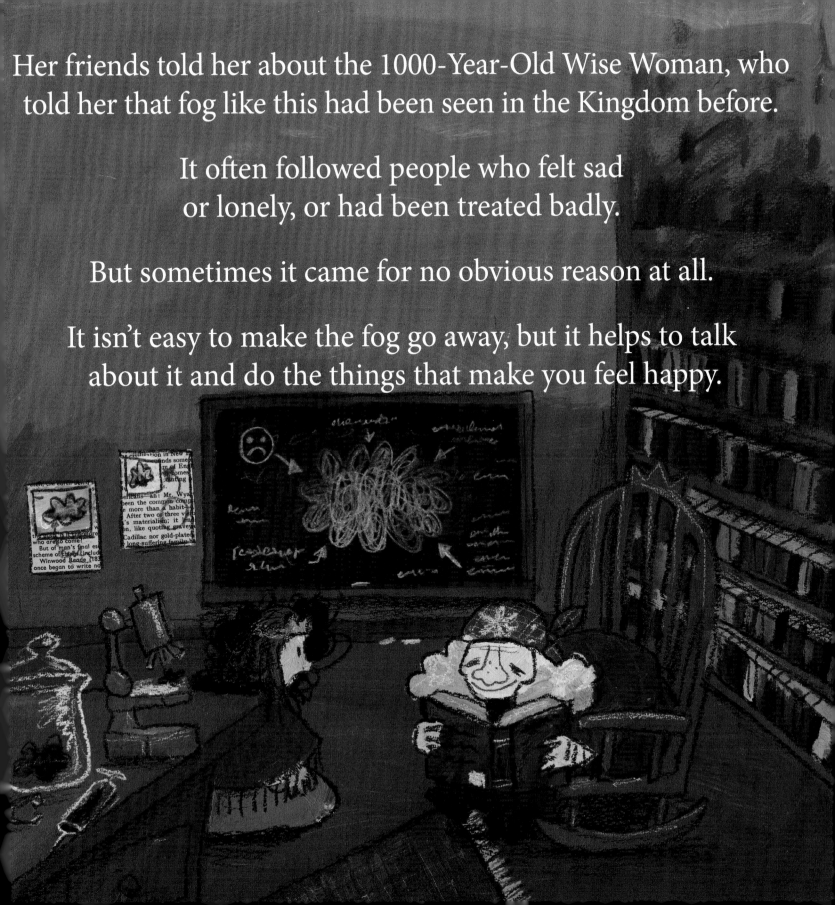

The Princess had no idea there were so many people in her life who would be willing to help her, or even just to listen to her when she needed to talk.

Suddenly she didn't feel so alone any more.

With all the help and support of
the people of the Kingdom, the fog
started to disappear, bit by bit,
just as gradually as
it had come.

Things started to go back to
normal after that.

Everyone was happy to see the Princess
back to her old self again.

But that's not the end of the story.

Every now and then, the dark clouds
would start to come back.

But when they did...

...she knew where to turn.

A Guide for Parents and Carers

Learning to cope with emotions is a normal part of children's development. Children will experience a range of emotions, including feelings of sadness that may be a very appropriate response to difficult situations they face. Periods of sadness or low mood are not uncommon and are often relatively short-lived. However, if they persist for a long time, are very overwhelming and impact on a child's daily life, it is important to explore this more carefully, to listen to the child's experiences and to provide extra support when needed.

Although depression in young children is relatively uncommon, periods of low mood can occur in this age group for a variety of reasons, and a small proportion of young children may go on to develop depression. Parents may detect changes in their child's mood and behaviour, for example children may seem bored and withdrawn, no longer showing interest in activities and hobbies they previously enjoyed. Parents may notice changes in their child's appetite or disturbances in their sleep pattern, and they may feel tired or lacking in energy a lot of the time. This can be accompanied by tearfulness and low self-esteem, feeling like they are 'no good'. Some children may be more irritable or agitated and have physical complaints, such as headaches and stomachaches. Depression in children can also be associated with increased anxiety, such as getting upset when apart from their parent or carer and being clingier.

Periods of low mood or depression may be triggered by a number of factors and can occur immediately following a stressful event or develop gradually over time. Events that cause disruption to a child's relationships or routine are common triggers, for example parental

separation or conflict, bereavement, illness in the child or family, and school problems such as bullying or friendship difficulties. Depression can run in families and children may be more vulnerable to developing depression if a parent or close family member suffers from depression or another mood disorder.

Parents and carers can help by listening to their child, helping to make sense of their experiences and develop ways of managing their feelings. They can also support their child to continue with activities which they enjoy or which give them a sense of achievement, and encourage them to spend time with friends and family. If parents or carers have further concerns, they should talk with their family doctor, who will be able to assess the difficulties in more detail and refer them on to other services if appropriate. This may include school-based counselling services or community mental health services, which are able to offer a more detailed assessment of the child's mood and discuss the treatment options available. This may involve counselling or talking therapies, such as cognitive behavioural therapy or family therapy.

This book is a helpful resource for parents and carers to open up conversations with children who are going through a period of low mood and encourage them to talk with a safe adult about how they feel. Children may also identify with the Princess in the book, helping them to feel less alone in their experiences.

Further information on child mental health can be found at www.youngminds.org.uk.

Melinda Edwards MBE, Consultant Clinical Psychologist
Dr Linda Bayliss, Highly Specialist Clinical Psychologist